The Girl Who Read To Birds

To Ashley—
Hope you enjoy!
♡ Julie

L.T. Godsmith Press

The Girl Who Read To Birds

By Michael Titus
Illustrated by Julie Miller

THE GIRL WHO READ TO BIRDS

ISBN: 978-0-9838212-0-5

First edition: August 2011
L.T. Godsmith Press

Book website: TheGirlWhoReadToBirds.com
Email: tgwrtb@gmail.com

Printed in the U.S.A.

For my Mother, who always knew.
For my Father, who always hoped.
For Molly Rae, forever my heart.
For Bwca, who would not have cared at all.

High above Avery Street, ribbons of dark birds chattered and circled. The exhilaration of flight was upon the large flock. It looked like skywriting in bird language. Several of the elder birds spiraled close to the ground, below the trees, past the leafy branches, as if they intended to land on the bowler hat that the child always wore.

"Avery!" called a shrill voice. Her mother. "Chores to do, Miss Fancy! And homework! I swear...wasting time staring at those birds..." The voice faded away, as Avery Street reluctantly pulled her gaze from the birds and walked toward the farmhouse.

Avery Street was twelve years old and a problem to her parents. She was a dreamer with her head in the clouds. This was not the way she was supposed to be, according to her parents. They did not bring her into this world to imagine, or indulge in fantasy; they brought her here to work hard and make something of herself. Something tangible. Something one could touch and hold and feel the weight of the thing. Something that meant something.

Avery was not a typical twelve year old. She was more stubborn than most children her age. She wore a bowler hat, even to school. She was eccentric, although she didn't know what that meant. Avery knew she was different. She couldn't get those birds out of her head. The birds were trying to communicate something to her. Something important.

The screen door slammed behind her as she dropped her backpack on the kitchen table.

"Child, take that silly hat off, " her mother chided. Avery did as she was told. "I swear," continued her mother, "I don't know what got into your father's head, giving you that hat. It's not suitable for a girl your age."

"I like it," replied Avery. "It was Grandpa's hat."

"Yes. An old man's hat. Your father's daddy already wore it out. No reason to keep it around, like most else in this house."

"But, Mama, it makes me feel good. Different. Like I'm part of Grandpa, somehow."

"You just mind who you are. Don't worry about your father or his father. They were both dreamers and that's the problem with this family. Wanting to be better than other folks. Big ideas. You see where those ideas went, don't you? In the garbage. Now you just go finish your homework."

"Yes, ma'am." Avery didn't bother to admit that she had no homework. Tomorrow was the last day of school. Then came the beloved summer break and the sweet freedom of birds and kites!

The screen door slammed a second time and her father came in. He was a tall man with calloused hands. Sometimes they were covered with grease. He had a part-time job as a mechanic, but mostly worked as a carpenter –

when he could find work. He was good with his hands, but times were tough. He also kept a garden and provided his family with fresh produce.

He took off his cap and wiped his sweaty brow. He slid his hand across his worn jeans before patting Avery on the head. "Well, what have we here?"

"Just an Avery," replied his daughter.

"Just? Well now. I reckon I see my little girl fixing to grow up and be somebody." He smiled. "Somebody important. Like a doctor."

"She's fixing to join the rest of family and be a failure the way she's on about spending her time with birds and daydreaming," her mother said. "Not

to mention keeping that ridiculous hat on her head. You'd think she didn't have any hair."

"It was Grandpa's hat," cried Avery. "He gave it to me! He said I was meant to keep it!"

Her father lost his smile.

"Girl, you watch your tone," he said. But there was a tinge of sadness in his voice. "I don't mean to speak ill of the dead, but your grandpa...he meant well, he did, to be sure. He was a good man, but he never amounted to much. He was a dreamer too, a poet..." Her father's voice faded, as he looked out the window. For a moment, it seemed he was somewhere else: another time, a different place. He was remembering his own childhood. His father had possessed a great imagination and had published books of poetry. But the family remained poor. Still, he'd inherited that ambition to live a creative life. He wrote. He failed, as his father had done before him. He wanted something better for Avery.

"Poetry doesn't put food on the table, child. There comes a time when you put the dreaming away and you go to work. It's all we have. It's called growing up."

Avery looked at her father's sunken face. "Then I don't want to grow up. Ever."

"And I don't want to be standing here washing dishes!" Her mother turned around and pointed her finger at her daughter. "But they won't wash themselves, will they?"

"You can wash dishes and still be a writer," Avery stated. "And do laundry and go shopping..."

" Not with your head in the clouds!"

"Now, Emma," her father interjected.

"Don't you 'Now, Emma' me! She's got to learn life is harsh!. If she doesn't make something of herself, she'll end up like us!" She immediately lowered her eyes, ashamed of what she'd spoken aloud. She wiped her soapy hands on her apron and turned away to hide the single tear that escaped her eye.

"We may be poor but we're not dead," whispered Avery. "Grandpa's the only one dead. He said there was more to life than..." Unable to complete the thought, she got up from the table and ran out of the kitchen.

Her father touched her mother's shoulder. "It'll be alright, Emma. Just you wait and see. Avery will be *this*."

"No, she'll be *that*." It was an old argument, never settled, never abandoned.

Avery ran outside, toward the fields, past the rows of corn. She ran as fast as she could, her arms stretched out, catching the wind. Her dark jacket was sliding off her shoulders and flapping like the outstretched wings of a crow leaving the earth. The birds appeared. They rushed past her, squawking. They taunted her, but urged her to keep going. She closed her eyes and ran on and on. She opened her eyes and saw the hill in front of her. She leaped, laughing, as the birds turned away to plunder the cornfield.

Finally! The last day of school! Avery stood outside, beside the mailbox on the dirt road, waiting for the long yellow bus. Her grandpa's bowler sat proudly on her head. Birds chirped in the nearby trees. She looked up and smiled. They were her friends, the only real ones she had.

A large crow flew low and nearly took away her bowler. She laughed. It was a ritual. The birds teased her, but they never snatched anything away. They weren't beyond stealing, being crows, but they never took from her.

The school bus pulled up with a hiss of dust. Avery sighed, walked up the steps and made her way past the other children. She sat, as always, by herself.

On most mornings, the other children would make fun of Avery, chiding her about the bowler or her "gypsy" clothing. But this being the last day before the summer break, they spared her the usual abuse. After all, the last day of school before summer is one of the best days in the world. There were more important things on everybody's mind.

A crow followed the bus.

At school, Avery went straight to homeroom. There would be no changing of classes today. The other teachers had all given their summer assignments to the homeroom teachers to pass round. Avery collected the papers that were passed down the row and stuck them in her notebook.

The teacher asked the students to get out one piece of paper and write about how they intended to spend the summer. Avery stared at her pencil. Her mind went blank. What she really wanted to do was write poems and stories. Could she put these taboo thoughts on paper? Would this get back to her parents? They argued enough about her. What could she write that her teacher might find acceptable?

She sighed and looked toward the window. It was raised slightly, because the day was exceptionally hot. A bird was perched there, silently. A crow. It was staring at her. She stared back, attempting to learn something from the silent Corvid.

But it stood on the sill, unmoving, like an antique resin ornament found on a mantel. Its eyes glittered like rhinestones.

Avery lost all sense of time. The paper in front of her remained blank.

The boy sitting behind her knocked the bowler off her head. The classroom filled with laughter.

As Avery bent over to retrieve her grandpa's hat, the boy said "Ha ha, Avery is bird-watching again! See?" He pointed to the open window. "Bird Girl, Bird Girl!" he intoned.

At this, the teacher glared at Avery. "What is going on? What is the meaning of this?" she exclaimed, just as the bell rang.

"Wait just a minute, class, " she said. She looked at the window and noticed the crow. "Shoo!" she yelled, running to the window and flapping her arms. "Shoo! Get out!" The crow cawed once and flew away. The teacher slammed the window down.

"Alright, class dismissed. All but Miss Street. Have a great summer, everybody!"

As the other children giggled and left the classroom, the teacher approached Avery's desk. She picked up Avery's paper and read the nothing that was there.

"Avery, you're such a good student. You make good grades. You can do something with your life. You have a gift for learning. But you don't concentrate. This paper is blank and it should be filled with your summer dreams." She sighed heavily. "You're just not conventional. I've tolerated that bowler hat out of respect for your grandfather. But no more. I don't want to see you in this school with this hat again. I'm going to inform the principal and I'm sending a note home to your parents. It's for your own good, my dear. I just want what's best for you."

As Avery, hat in hand, stuffed the teacher's letter into her backpack, she felt a tingle near her scalp. She reached with her free hand to scratch the itch and found a crow feather tangled in her thick, wavy hair. She glanced once more at the closed window. The crow was gone.

Summertime.

No school. No shoes or socks. The grass tickled bare feet. Freedom. Tire-swings. Lazy days with the best of all to be doing – nothing. At night, the open window let the cool evening breeze whisper round the curtains and you were sent to sleep by a lullaby of crickets and frogs.

Summertime – and the living is easy. Avery had once been walking past the barn and heard her father singing. He thought he was alone and Avery didn't want to let on she'd heard the brief sound of something rare in his voice, something light and almost...cheerful.

The living wasn't so easy for Avery. It wasn't like a death in the family, but it sure wasn't a swirl-in-a-summer-skirt picnic either. It was just life. Avery knew her parents worked hard for what they had and what they gave to her, and she was grateful. She also realized that some kids in her school had a much worse existence, a tougher life with few opportunities.

Avery thought a lot about opportunities. The problem was that between her parents and her teachers, nobody ever thought about asking her what she wanted from her one life. Her future was mapped out in the cartography of other people's desires. She would go on to college and become *this* or *that*. There was no argument. No wavering from these two careers. She had no voice in this decision. When she tried to speak up, she was told to "just listen to those who know what's best for you," and that was the end of the conversation.

First day of summer vacation and Avery was climbing the stairs to the attic. She hadn't been to the attic in years. It was the last place anyone would think to look for her. Probably full of dirt and dust and spiders. At least there was a window. She could open it to let some of the mildew and dank attic smell out.

The attic door opened with a ghostly creak, as if to say "Welcome back, stranger, I've been waiting for you!" It was obvious the attic was not the most popular room in the old farmhouse. For a moment, Avery almost felt sorry for it. Then she opened the door wide and peered inside.

The dust danced in the sunbeams streaming through the one oval window. All else was shuttered by shadows. Avery walked further in and pulled the string to light the dangling bulb.

As her eyes adjusted to the new illumination, she abruptly found herself in a magical realm. "Oh. My. God." she uttered, looking through the latticework of cobwebs.

This was her parents' pirate treasure! Plunder from a lifetime of silence and shush, hidden away from all avaricious eyes! Here there be Paradise! Unconsciously, she brushed aside the spider's handiwork and peered deeper into this precious vault.

There were two dressmaker's mannequins, one leaning against the other. Headless twins chattering about times gone by. An old metal fan hung above them, as if it wished it could still offer comfort from the sticky heat. Avery had to navigate around a series of wooden boxes to go further. On another wall was a shelf of porcelain dolls, in varying stages of decay. One of them sat in a wicker rocking chair. She seemed to be the eldest, but her dust-brown hair showed traces of black, from a time when she was young and lived in a better room, with a tiny china tea-set and a child nearby.

There was also a row of life-sized, stick-like figures with shocks of straw hair. Several of them sported tattered hats. Avery laughed. These were her father's failed attempts at constructing a working scarecrow. He couldn't make them appear very menacing and, besides, the crows around here had always been alert to his fruitless project.

In another corner, Avery found a stack of framed paintings, one of them quite large. It was an oil painting of her great-great Aunt Lena. It was so ponderous that there was nowhere to hang it. She flipped through some of the other paintings. Some looked, like Lena, as if they were her ancestors, but she couldn't place them.

One painting stood out. It leaned against a trunk on the floor. It was her grandpa. She touched the quizzical brow, ran her fingers across his mustache, yellow from years of smoking a pipe. She could still remember the apple-tinted aroma of his tobacco. His eyes twinkled merrily, with a hint of his usual mischief. His mouth was frozen in a wry smile, not quite happy, not quite sad. She leaned over and kissed his wrinkled forehead, not minding the dust that glazed her lips.

With tears in her eyes, Avery moved Grandpa away from the trunk, setting him gently down, facing her. She wouldn't need any reminder to take him with her when she was finished here. There was plenty of space downstairs for Grandpa and she had no intention of leaving without him.

Avery sat down on the trunk and looked at the painting of Grandpa opposite her. She put her palms on her cheek, realizing that she wasn't getting any work done — at least not the kind of work her parents would consider chores.

The more she stared at Grandpa, the more he stared back.

His eyes appeared to be animated, glancing down. Avery looked down. Dirt plank flooring. She looked to her right. An ancient vacuum tube radio. To her left, her old red wagon in which she used to haul stones gathered from the creek side. Up: more cobwebs, abandoned by their spinners. Down again: nothing else but...the trunk she was sitting on.

She sighed, stood up, turned around, and knelt by the trunk. It wasn't locked. It looked like it hadn't ever been opened. There was probably nothing in it. But Avery couldn't resist undoing the latch and lifting the lid.

Notebooks. The trunk was half-full of bound notebooks and some flotsam papers. Ignoring the handwritten papers for the moment, she picked up one of the notebooks and opened it. Her eyes grew as wide as those of the derelict scarecrows.

These were her father's books. Books of stories and poetry. Not just books her father must have collected and read, but books her father had, before she was even born, written!

Nobody had ever mentioned this. No one had warned her. Her father was a writer! How could they keep this from her, knowing how much she loved to read! She fell back on the floor with one of the manuscripts in her hands. Slowly she opened it and began to read. It was a story about the world of faerie and the denizens within. She read for a bit and picked up another

journal. It was full of poems, some of them written to her mother, others sang about his life, his childhood, his dreams.

Why were they abandoned? These stories, poems, dreams? These words told the tale of a father she didn't know, a wholly different man she never had the chance to meet. Who was he really? And why were these wondrous stories buried in the attic?

There were no answers. The scarecrows continued to grin. The dolls' faces looked blank. The headless mannequins were content to sleep. At the oval window a crow cawed once, then took flight.

Avery knew that she'd discovered an enormous treasure, but she was brought back to earth by the fact that her chores would not get themselves done without her help. She tucked several of her father's journals under her coat, put her grandpa's painting underneath her arm and went downstairs to her room.

Avery hid Grandpa in her closet, until she could decide where to display him. Then she carried her father's stories to the big oak tree on top of the hill. As she began to read, she didn't notice the birds flying in, gathering on the limbs of the oak, expanding the shade with their bodies and outstretched wings, nor the multitude of other silent birds making their way toward her like a storm cloud.

She devoured the first fairy tale quickly. Luckily, her father had excellent penmanship, so she didn't have to squint to decipher the sentences. It was about a land of tall weeds. The weeds, like everything else in the story, could talk. They didn't want to be considered mere "weeds." Thus, they sent an envoy to the flower kingdom to petition their king. Then there was a battle which neither kingdom won. It was a sad tale, in a way. No "happily ever after." She pondered the meaning of this.

As she closed the book and leaned back against the old oak, she noticed something very peculiar.

She was completely surrounded by birds.

The branches of the oak were dark with crows, ravens and starlings. On the ground, in close circles, were robins, jays and little hopping wrens. They were staring at her. No, Avery realized: they were staring at the book. She looked up. Past yellow beaks, black eyes peered down.

"Hullo," she ventured. A crow cawed.

"Pleasantly odd day, isn't it?" She couldn't think of anything else to add.
Two crows cawed.

It seemed as if they were trying to talk to her. But they weren't weeds. And this wasn't a story. This was real. Avery wasn't afraid, although her imagination was busy telling her to get up, run back to the farmhouse and shut the windows.

Avery shook her head. She loved birds and now here she was talking to them. "I'm talking to birds," she admitted. Three crows cawed and a raven squawked. The little wrens continued to hop about and then began a chorus of chirping so persistent that even the crows fell silent.

"Whoa! Calm down there! I didn't bring any food with me. Not even a breadcrumb."

At this, the birds, every single one, squawked, chirped and cawed with a cacophonous fluttering of wings. A feather drifted down and settled on the brim of Avery's bowler. The noise was nearly deafening.

Avery put her hands over her ears and the book she'd been holding to her chest fell on her outstretched legs and opened. The noise rushed away. All the birds immediately hushed.

No, thought Avery. It couldn't be.

Tentatively, she closed the book. The birds resumed their raucous orchestrations.

She opened the book quickly. Silence returned. She could even hear bees buzzing in the clover.

"You...you want me to read to you?" asked Avery, peering up and down and all around. A single wren took flight, perched upon her shoulder and chirped gently in response.

"You do! That's what you're all crying about!" The birds in the trees cocked their heads. The birds on the ground moved closer. "What I did on my summer vacation!" exclaimed Avery, laughing. "Well, nobody will believe it, but that doesn't mean it didn't happen." She smiled at the birds. "Remember, you guys asked for it."

She turned to the second story. It was about a handsome, but sad, man who wanted to be kissed by a beautiful princess so he could be turned back into a turtle.

"Once upon a time..."

From that point on, Avery's passion was to find time in each day to go and sit under the old oak and read aloud to the birds. They listened eagerly, hungrily. This was turning out to be the best summer ever. Avery had never been so happy.

One day, several weeks later, her father was looking out from the kitchen window. You can't sit under a large tree on a hill, surrounded by a sea of birds, and expect no one to notice. He called for his wife. They both looked at their daughter and the birds, although they couldn't see what she was doing.

"That's our Avery!" cried Mother.

"None other," replied Father. "We sure didn't have twins, as far as I recollect."

"What on earth is going on out there?" asked Mother, ignoring her husband's last remark. "All those...those...birds! What do they want? Why are they out there? Do you reckon she's in danger? So many birds...I've never seen the like..."

"I don't hear any screaming," replied Father. "I don't suppose she's doing anything but just sitting there, enjoying the weather."

"This is no time for your old foolishness. We need to get her back inside the house and find out what on earth is going on out there!"

"Now, Emma," said Father, turning around. "I don't see the harm in this. For now. Avery doesn't keep anything from us. You know that. Give her some time and she'll let us in on her secret, if that's what it is. She's been doing her chores and hasn't been a bit of trouble lately."

"Well, maybe you're right. I just don't like it. I'll give her a day or two. No more."

As it turned out, Avery was not forthcoming about her adventures with the birds. How could she tell her parents that she was reading to them? And reading from her father's old journals? They wouldn't understand. She wanted to tell them everything, about how the birds actually wanted to hear these stories, but who would believe her? As she lay in bed, watching a bird at the window, she found it hard to believe this was really happening. Sometimes she imagined herself a character in one of her father's fables, wondering what "the end" would be. And if anything came after that part.

A few more days passed. Though her parents didn't forget about Avery and the birds, they were preoccupied with running a farm and working wherever there was work to be done. One evening, Avery's mother walked into her daughter's room. She sighed. The child hadn't made her bed. She set about straightening the covers and fluffing the pillows. That's when she found it. The journal. It was tucked beneath the one of the pillows.

She drew a deep breath. She knew exactly what it was. She sat down on Avery's bed, opened it, and began to read. Just before the tears started to flow, she snapped the book shut and carried it downstairs.

Avery was outside feeding the chickens. Father was lingering over dinner, as there had been no call for him at the garage that day. Suddenly his journal fell from behind his shoulder, landing on the table with a resounding thunk that made the coffee in his cup quiver.

He pulled his hand away as if burnt, turned around and looked at his scowling wife. "Why, Emma? Why would you do this?"

"I wouldn't. Didn't. I found this just now under Avery's pillow."

"How did she get hold of it?"

"I reckon she found it while snooping in the attic. I'd forgotten that trunk was still up there. Little Miss Nosy took this, and heaven only knows what else."

"I always meant to get rid of that old trunk. Don't know why I didn't."

"I know." She patted her husband on the back. "Just one of those things that slipped our mind. We can't think of everything. No sense blaming ourselves about it now. We'll have to have a talk with her."

"I know." His head sank. "I know." He shook his head, as if trying to clear it of the distant words he'd once created. "Call her in, Emma. Let's get it over with."

Avery was summoned. She walked into the living room, where her parents waited. She smiled. That smile quickly vanished as she noticed the journal her father was holding in his hand, like a scolding puppet.

"Care to explain this, young lady." It wasn't a question.

"I found it in the attic, in your old trunk," replied Avery, shifting her weight from one foot to the other.

"Ah. So you just took it, then."

"Yes."

"Without asking."

"Yes, but..."

Her father cut her explanation short. "Avery, this is what we would call stealing."

"No! I..."

Father held up his hand. "It wasn't yours to take," he explained.

Avery was heartbroken. She'd never stolen anything. "But Daddy! Those stories are so full of beauty and life!" She began to cry. "What if I'd never got to read any of them?"

"That's the whole point," her mother said. "You were never meant to."

"But why?"

Her mother buried her head in her hands as she sat on the couch. She rubbed her face and looked up at her daughter. "Avery," she began, in a gentle voice, "your father inherited some odd notions from your grandpa. He believed he could write and it would make him happy. We'd earn a decent living from our dreams. Yes, I was part of it. I encouraged your father. We sacrificed. We scrimped and saved but we still lost our first home, before you were born. We lost everything."

"We tried to do what our hearts told us, Avery," her father interrupted. "But nobody would even read the stories, let alone buy them."

"And so we ended up in debt," continued her mother. "Just like your grandpa before us. We learned a hard lesson. We learned that all this art was for nothing. It didn't bring us anything. It didn't put food on the table. It wasn't real work."

"Then you came along," said her father. "Avery, it's fine to dream. But your dreams don't take you anywhere but down. So we put aside those childish fancies and went to work. Real work. Work that paid. Do you understand?"

Avery didn't know what to say to this. Her dreams were all she had. Was she dreaming the birds, who gathered in great numbers to listen to her voice? Was everything just a series of dreams, all of them bad, like this moment? If that was the truth, then what was left to look forward to?

"No," she admitted.

"Dreams drain the spirit, baby," said her father.

"You're only twelve," her mother chimed in. "One day you'll be all grown up. Too fast, I'll admit, but then you'll look back and know that we set you straight."

"Or maybe I'll know what you really thought of Grandpa and Daddy's stories," sobbed Avery. "Maybe I'll want my own life, not yours!"

"Avery!" cried her parents.

"I'm going to be just like Grandpa, no matter what. You wait and see!"

"You will NOT!" cried her mother. She looked at her husband. "Well?"

Avery's father got up and took his daughter by the hand. "Come with me." He led her up to the attic, to the forbidden trunk. He opened it and placed his old journal back with the other papers and notebooks and closed the lid. Then he put a padlock on the hasp of the trunk and clicked it tight.

"That's the end of this nonsense, Avery," he said. He put the key in his pocket.

Avery began to cry. "But the birds..."

"Yes, what about all those birds?" asked her mother.

"They liked those stories. I read to them. They listened."

"Avery," said her father, "birds don't care. Nobody cares."

"I do," she wept, "and they did. They did!"

"See what this foolishness has caused?" said her mother. "Reading to birds. Odd notions. Quirky behavior. I believe we might have to take her to the doctor!"

"It's not that bad, Emma. Just a passing fad. All kids have them. It's over and done with now."

"It's not over!" cried Avery, as she ran back downstairs.

"What are we going to do with that child?" asked Mother.

"Nothing. Now." replied Father. "She'll get over it. Just like we did. She's young yet. She'll forget. I'll go check on her."

He put his hands in his pockets and sadly walked down the steps.

Emma's eyes filled with tears, for all of them. "You were a good writer," she said softly, glancing at the trunk. "A poet..."

Avery's father pushed open the door to her room. She was lying on the bed, her face buried in her pillow, sobbing softly. He looked at her open window. Three crows perched on the sill, watching her as well. Then they turned their gaze on him. He took a step backward, almost fearful at first,

but then he saw something in their large inky eyes. He saw color. He saw the old oak tree. He saw Avery. He felt a strange feeling emanating from those eyes. Within his buried poet's heart, he knew this feeling. It was remorse.

He wondered if they could see that same feeling reflected in his own eyes.

Not knowing what else to do, he gently closed Avery's door and left her alone with her birds.

Avery fell asleep. She tossed and turned through the night. She dreamed she was flying over the farm, over the old oak, into a sweet blue smudge of endless sky.

The crows kept watch until morning. With the sunrise, they fluttered off as one, whispering to each other in flight.

A lingering hush fell over the Street family the next morning. Breakfast was taken in silence. Avery left to get her chores done. Her father left to go to the garage. Her mother remained to clean up and then started work on a quilt for her daughter. She thought about adding patches of birds. She hadn't made up her mind about that yet.

Avery finished her chores quickly. She knew she didn't do as thorough a job as usual, but she didn't care. At lunch, she merely picked at her food as her mother watched nervously. Then she walked out to the old oak tree, sat down and stared at her empty hands. The birds were already there.

Avery looked up and around her. She could feel the ache in their hearts. They were greedy for stories, and she'd brought nothing for them. A wren landed on her knee and chirped pleadingly. She held out her finger. The little bird jumped up and perched there, its face turned slightly to the side. It was perplexed and Avery could do nothing to alleviate its confusion.

She drew the wren closer to her face and smiled. "You're cute." The wren chirped again, cocking its head in the opposite direction, as if merrily chiding her. "Don't tease me. The stories are gone, taken away. It's not my fault. Maybe I could just make up some of my own..."

A crow cawed from above.

"Well, how would you know? You just might be surprised at..." She stopped in mid-sentence. Her thoughts were like a beginning juggler's apples – dropped. She mentally tried to pick up those fallen apples but her brain couldn't reach them. She abruptly stood up and the wren cackled away.

"Would you mind repeating that?" Avery asked, looking up at the crow, beyond all expectation. After all, she hadn't slept well the night before.

The crow cawed again and added several extra notes.

Avery was spellbound. "You do? I can? You will?" she blurted out.

The crow yapped away and another joined in.

"Yes," replied Avery, "yes...I would love that, if you please. I mean, if you don't mind."

The crows cawed, a raven squawked and the wrens squeaked.

She understood them. Avery understood every single word the birds uttered. She didn't know how this was possible, but then she never considered if they understood what she read to them. She thought they just liked the

sound of a human voice. It never occurred to her that they'd learned human speech and that, by some sort of osmosis — was that the right word? Or magic? Miracle? — she had absorbed theirs! Despite how terrible yesterday had been, this was a completely new day, and the best possible outcome of any day she could imagine!

She sat back down, as the birds instructed — the Raven admonished them to not all speak at once — and listened. The crow told her that they'd always understood human language, but had never yet found anyone willing to converse with them. All they knew about people they gathered from watching and listening. At first, they'd thought humans a rather boring lot, until they discovered libraries filled with books. They wondered what humans wrote about but, as clever as they were, couldn't decipher the written word. This was the gift Avery had given to them. The birds immediately sensed her love of these tales and adored the sound of her soft voice as she read aloud to them.

The birds admitted that they had listened rapturously to these products of the human imagination — which they hadn't believed even existed. They lived for stories. They had volumes of their own but, since they were unable to write, these were passed on by the oral tradition — told to the young by the elders.

They were saddened by the fact that the human stories had been taken away from them — and from Avery. Now, they wished to repay her for her kindness. Now, they would recite their stories to her. She was asked to sit and listen. She did as she was bidden.

One of the crows began to recite a story to her. It was otherworldly to Avery, being avian in nature and never told to a human being before. She basked in the glorious new telling of their unknown fables until darkness fell. She walked back to the farmhouse changed. The Avery of this morning was quite a different Avery now. She didn't feel her feet touch the ground all the way home.

Her parents let her go to bed without much fuss. They'd been worried about her and wondered if they were being too harsh with her. She was only twelve. All children had imagination, didn't they? Perhaps they should leave her alone. Let her be herself. You are only given one childhood and that ought to be nurtured and celebrated. That didn't mean you favored them with false hope and lies, though. Even children needed to know the truth about life, so they could prepare for what it was going to throw their way.

For the next few days, Avery was left to herself. She did her chores. She conversed with her parents.

Every afternoon, she went to the old oak tree and listened to the birds tell her their strange, yet oddly familiar, tales. It was often difficult for her to imagine that she was part of this new life, this world of the birds, but she had never felt so alive, so magnificent in her own earthbound skin. Now she knew the windswept movement of bone-covered wings, the perching on high towers, the gatherings in trees, the stealing of corn and rye, the aerial glee and the playful haunts of the flock.

But summer, even for a child, cannot last forever.

Avery's parents were concerned by her gradual absence from the family and her dependence upon the birds. Finally, they confronted her.

"Avery," began her father, "those birds of yours."

"Oh," replied Avery. "They're my friends."

"Your friends?" continued her mother. "What do you mean, child?"

"Well..." Avery admitted, "they talk to me."

"They do what?' asked her father.

"They talk to me," Avery tried to explain. "Remember when I used to read to them? Well, I can't now. So they tell me their own stories."

"What do you mean?" asked her mother, warily.

"They talk to me. I understand them."

"You...you understand what the birds are saying?" continued mother.

"Yes," answered Avery. "It's like talking to somebody from another country, really. You just have to listen and practice and learn."

"Avery," said her father, "it's not like a foreign language. We're talking about a different species!"

"Dear," said Mother, "people can't talk to birds or any other animal.

Are you feeling poorly?"

"I've never felt better, Mother. Do you know what birds do at their funerals?"

"That's enough, Avery!" Father said. "We've given you great leeway this summer. But this has got to end!"

"It's got to end, for certain," Mother chimed in. "It's not normal! You think this is real!"

"It is real, Mama," exclaimed Avery, "I could tell you about..."

"This is all about your grandpa!" said Mother. "This is his influence and it's time to finally put an end to it!"

"But Grandpa..." began Avery.

"He was the one all this craziness came from!" cried Mother. "We need to get back to being a normal family! I just can't stand living like this again..."

"Your mother's right, Avery," Father said. "You've gone too far with this talking to birds stuff. It does sound like your grandpa. He's gone, and so are his fantasies. Now it's time you put these crazy thoughts away too. Give me that hat."

"But this is all I left of Grandpa!" Avery implored.

"I think that's the lesson here, Child," said Mother.

Avery's mother removed the old hat from her head and handed it to Father with trembling hands. "I'm sorry about this, Avery," he said, as he carried it up to the attic. He placed the hat upon his chest of forgotten writings, then closed and locked the attic door. He added this key to his pocket. A tear slid down his cheek. "There," he said. "The last of my father is locked away."

It is a common mistake to think that children cannot suffer depression. Avery experienced it now for the first time. She was distraught, unable to think or to feel. But she felt that the connection between her and Grandpa was lost forever with the taking of the bowler. She knew it was just a hat, but it had been special. It was not a charm or amulet, imbued with magical powers; it was a sweet remembrance of the one person who would understand her, believe in her as that strange and separate entity we call "our own self." It was a self that belonged to no other and never would. It was once only.

She moped all day, lost and abandoned. It hurt so much that her parents didn't believe her. When had she ever lied? It hurt even more that the birds had made themselves scarce. No chirping of wrens or cawing of crows. Not a bird in sight anywhere near the oak or in the sky that slowly turned to orange slices of dusk.

She walked in the far field, having wept her way there with a fierceness that left her eyes too dry to make more tears. She felt that summer had forever ended but, for once, nobody had sent a note home explaining its abrupt termination.

An odd feeling invaded her feet. She kicked at a stone. Perhaps she'd wandered too far from home. But that couldn't be. She knew these fields as well as she knew all the rooms in the farmhouse. Still, her feet tingled, then began to ache slightly. She turned around to survey her path. There was the farmhouse. There was the oak tree – distant, but she could still make out all the familiar landmarks.

Finally, she saw two crows returning to the oak tree. They dropped to the ground for an instant and then perched on a spindly branch.

It should be dark, shouldn't it? Yes, she could feel the dark, like a whinnying horse, attempting to gallop through the cat's-eyed gauze of Dusk. Dusk, however, refused to budge. *Wait,* it seemed to say to impatient Nightfall, *give us a little more time this one day and we will repay you in kind.* The Night relented: *I will make this trade with you, but I cannot wait long.*

Though it was warm and humid, Avery shivered. She began to let the remaining light lead her back, back to the old oak. The path was clear and she didn't stumble, although she thought it quite possible, considering the growing numbness of her feet. It had now climbed to her ankles.

One foot in front of the other. Steady, now.

Avery made it to the old oak and slumped to her knees by the trunk, on the side of the tree that sloped down from the bank to the small creek.

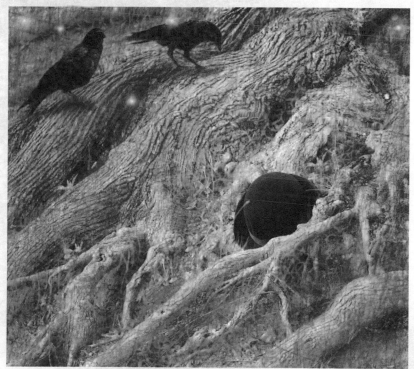

She looked at the base of the tree, where the ancient roots had broken free of the hard earth, the emerging tendrils heavy with bark and moss, bones shattering dirt-skin that could never hold them within such weak confines. In the ribcage of the roots lay her bowler hat.

Avery felt weak, but she reached for the hat, touched the brim to assure herself it was real. She picked it up, smelled the old pipe-tobacco, earth and sweat cologne that she knew so well. She placed it on her head.

How...?

The crows! As lovable as they were mischievous – there were no better thieves in the world. They smirked at closed windows and cackled deliciously in the presence of locks. They knew the tricks that would put any human robber to shame. Hide-and-seek was their stock-in-trade; they played the game with unstinting enthusiasm – and they always won. The more difficult the prize, the greater their glee in fetching it away.

They'd never stolen from her, but now they'd stolen for her.

Avery had no idea how she was going to explain this to her parents.

Dusk was still holding fast to its last night-bargained moments. Avery saw that the crows were not alone. The entire tree filled with birds again. Hundreds of birds. All silent, all intently watching her, as she attempted to stand. The numbness had spread to her legs. She struggled but stood.

"Thank you," she whispered, looking up at the crows. "Thank you for this kindness. For being here, especially now."

A large Raven flew down from the top of the tree and landed on a branch close to her face. He didn't need to wear a crown. His authority was understood by all, including Avery.

"This can be stopped," he said, "before it travels beyond our ability to hold it. It need go no further."

Avery tried to respond to this, but the words flew away from her breath, a voiceless, winged utterance.

"Do you know all that we require of you?" asked the Raven.

Avery nodded. She knew. She was hesitant, but she knew. She wasn't being coerced into anything; she was being given a choice, a different and uneasy future.

"There can be no turning back, Child," the Raven said, with a tinge of pity in his voice. "Think carefully, although there is little time left."

I have given you much, the Night airily sang, *it is time to reclaim my own.*

In an instant, all of Avery's memories — from childhood till this very moment — breached from the sea of her dreams: all of the good and the bad, the forgotten and the yet-to-be. The encroaching numbness now rested in her belly.

She nodded.

"What is done is done," stated the Raven. He flew back up into the high branches, unseen, as Dusk prepared for sleep.

Then the birds fell.

They dropped from their perches like stones: dark, voiceless as Avery, like arrows shot from the heart of a taut bowstring, wings folded, plummeting.

Hundreds of these bird-stones plunged upon Avery Street, releasing their thin air-boned feathers, stopping just short of the fatal earth. They covered her feet and spun around her ankles, circling her body in a blurry hurricane until she could not be seen, and still they gathered momentum and spun round her so wildly that even the Night was startled and stopped its pace.

They whirled like steam from all horizons of the world, until they were one great mass. The clouds passed quickly overhead, as if fearful they'd be caught in the freakish maelstrom.

The little wren who once perched on Avery's finger broke the silence with a single chirp. The bird-storm ended.

The exhausted birds made their way back to the branches of the oak tree, panting, drained, forever changed. They were tired but sleepless. They

would remember this day all their short lives. They would recite this epic tale to their young, so it would never be forgotten.

For her part, Avery would never forget. She'd also changed.

Avery Street was a crow. A delicate and small crow, but a Corvid nonetheless, even though a small bowler hat adorned her head. This was the Raven's gift to her. An alteration. A turning point. A transmogrification into what she'd desired all her life, but only realized at the moment when she gave her permission freely.

It seemed so natural, so inevitable. She was comfortable in her clothing of feather, thick-pointed claws grasping a branch and all the air she could imagine within her bones and the ever- swelling sky. She chittered and tested her wings. It was strange at first, this business of flying, although she'd often dreamed of it. The other birds clucked at her initial clumsiness. This was their way of cheering her on.

She'd have to find a new vocabulary to describe her first flight in a manner that the other birds could grasp.

Avery stretched into the night sky, said hello to the full moon, closed her eyes and let the faint breeze make a path for this exuberance, this abundance. Her innate senses took her round and round the oak tree, but this excursion was tiring to a newly-winged creature. There would be much for her to get used to. She perched among the other crows and spoke to them in their language. The other Corvids did not have to explain the details to her. For once, she fully understood her role in the world.

She would be, as long as she lived, the gatekeeper. The teller of tales in both languages. Avery realized she could not retain the longevity that she would as a human. She would make this sacrifice.

But what about her parents? Besides Grandpa, who was already gone, they were the only humans she loved. They would miss her and be terribly sad. She was determined to let them know.

Avery left the tree and flew back to the farmhouse. There would be at least one open window.

Her parents always enjoyed the night's cool breeze drifting in. It settled them. It was always the delicious end to another day, before another tumultuous tomorrow began.

Avery found the parlor window raised. She perched on the sill.

Her parents were sitting on the small sofa. Mother was knitting. Father was humming a soft tune to himself.

"Where's Avery?" he asked. "I haven't seen her all day."

"I haven't seen her, either," replied Mother. "But it's dark out. Time for her to be in bed. You ought to call her in."

Her father turned to the open window to yell to his daughter. His mouth opened to speak to the yard, where he imagined his daughter must be playing. Then he saw the bird. A crow on the sill, wearing a tiny bowler hat. The crow looked at him with an abiding love.

"No." he said.

"Well, if you won't get her inside, I will," Mother said.

"No," repeated Father.

"What on earth has possessed you?" asked Mother, looking up from her knitting. She followed her husband's gaze and saw the little crow.

"No," she gasped, dropping her skein of yarn. "It's not right. It can't be!" She laughed. "It's been such a long day..."

"My god, Emma. It can be. It is." Father choked up. "Those eyes. Her eyes..."

"Now don't be silly, dear," replied Mother. "Please don't be...crazy. Shoo that crow away. It's time for Avery to come in."

But they both looked long at the little crow on the windowsill, saw the little bowler hat on its head, saw the tears in its eyes and they knew. Parents always recognize their children, regardless of form.

"Oh, Avery!" wept Mother.

"My baby!" wept Father.

Avery wept along with them. Then she let out a deep sigh and told them everything that had happened to her and why.

"But they can change you back!" said Mother, after listening to the tale.

"What's done is done," replied Avery, quoting the Raven. "It can't be undone. I'm so sorry."

"You're gone to us, then," said Father in a low, stunned voice.

"No, Daddy, never gone. I'll be here every evening. I'll tell you the stories of the birds and you can write them down, if you want. I'll never really leave home."

Avery's parents didn't know what to think. The impossible had come to visit, unannounced and unbidden. They were losing a daughter and gaining what? A crow? A bird-child? But they could no longer deny her any wish that she asked of them. They loved her dearly, as she loved them.

"As long I live, I will never leave you," whispered Avery.

"As long as we live, we'll always be near," replied her parents.

Avery flew off, back to the old oak. She still had much to learn from her new friends.

But as long as the farmhouse stood, she spent every evening on the windowsill and, eventually, inside. She remained a bird-child. Her parents accepted this new reality and eagerly awaited her visits.

It was sad and it was joyous, as all life proves to be. On Emma's urging, Avery's father retrieved his old journals and notebooks from the attic. He read them aloud to Avery and she memorized them, so she could tell them to the birds.

He also continued to write new stories until the day he passed away, pen in hand.

Emma made sure that these still unpublished stories were known to her daughter.

Emma died two days before her daughter fell out of the sky.

The birds mourned.

In the vast library of the universe, the book of starlight was opened by a child who wanted nothing more than to read to the birds. They loved all stories and had many of their own to share by song – but, until Avery was born, none to speak back by the voice they loved best – the human one.

The birds gathered round and their ears opened to tales they would later relate to their young, in their own language.

Though the myths would change with each telling, they would never fade away. The Book would not be silent. The child, Avery, was just one chapter. The birds were the words.

Each individual life was a paragraph.

The End.

Acknowledgements

Many people were involved in making this book – making it work, and making it worthwhile to have written. First, I must offer my undying gratitude to my friend and illustrator, Julie Miller, who was in the trenches from the beginning. Julie brought this book to life with her inimitable magic. Colleen Anderson, of "Mother Wit Writing and Design," was the first person that gave the manuscript a good going over with her dancing red pencil – and improved it greatly. Megan Gainer, the first "outsider" who read the manuscript and called me in tears to express her love for the story. At that moment, I needed those tears of joy. My family gave me so much support; I'd have been lost many years ago without them. My cats Grendl, Bwca (RIP), Marley, and Hobbes gave me blessed companionship – and solitude – when I needed it. Finally there is you, dear reader. Thank you for taking this journey with me.

– Michael Titus

My dear friend Michael, I wouldn't be thanking a soul if not for your wondrous tale of courage and magic. I'm honored to have made this journey with you. We certainly got knocked around a bit, but we're stronger for it. Many, many thanks also to the brilliant and beautiful Eveshka "Peanut" Guranich for being so perfect for the part of Avery, and for so willingly doing crazy things to make these images perfect. You are Avery; it was meant to be. Also, thank you to Paul and Georgie Guranich for allowing me access to your amazing daughter and for posing with her in a number of images. You have an wondrous family, and it was a pleasure working with all of you. Big thanks also go out to Ashok ☐ hosla (*aka amkhosla on Flickr*) and Les (*aka glacierman on Flickr*) for allowing me to use your otherworldly bird photos. You two are astounding photographers, and I'm honored to have worked with such gorgeous images. The illustrations in this book would not have been possible without them. Thanks also to Allison "T.S." Bradley for being our proofreader extraordinaire. Finally, I'd like to thank my husband, Bill, for being my props handler, my lighting director, my scene scouter, my spirit lifter and my constant support. You're my best friend and I love you.

– Julie Miller

Photo by Ashok Khosla

MICHAEL TITUS lives with his three cats, including one who is a ghost, surrounded by the hauntingly beautiful mountains of rural West Virginia. He is fond of coffee and tea, and collects small, tin, wind-up toy robots and bowler hats. He is currently writing his second book.

JULIE MILLER graduated from Tyler School or Art, Temple University with a BFA in painting and art history. After this, because of her passion for the sciences, she went back to school and studied cytology at Thomas Jefferson University. She uses her visual skills to analyze human cells through a microscope in a pathology lab as well as to create artwork in her home studio. She is currently working on a few new books and living happily in Pennsylvania with her husband and two dogs. You can find more of her artwork at **HaggisVitae.com**.

9128677R0

Made in the USA
Charleston, SC
13 August 2011